Eat Your Peas

To Claire, Elliott and Jack
K.G.
To the Sullivans
N.S.

EAT YOUR PEAS
A RED FOX BOOK 978 1 862 30804 6
First published in Great Britain by The Bodley Head,
an imprint of Random House Children's Books,
A Random House Group Company

The Bodley Head edition published 2000
Red Fox edition published 2001
This edition published 2009

1 3 5 7 9 10 8 6 4 2

Text copyright © Kes Gray, 2000
Illustrations copyright © Nick Sharratt, 2000

The right of Kes Gray and Nick Sharratt to be identified as the author and illustrator of this
work has been asserted in accordance with the Copyright, Designs and Patents Act 1988.

Red Fox Books are published by Random House Children's Books,
61–63 Uxbridge Road, London W5 5SA

www.daisyclub.co.uk

Addresses for companies within The Random House Group Limited can be found at:
www.randomhouse.co.uk/offices.htm

THE RANDOM HOUSE GROUP Limited Reg. No. 954009

A CIP catalogue record for this book is available from the British Library.

Printed in China

Eat Your Peas

Kes Gray & Nick Sharratt

RED FOX

It was dinner time again and Daisy just knew what her mum was going to say, before she even said it.
"Eat your peas," said Mum.

Daisy looked down at the little green balls
that were ganging up on her plate.
"I don't like peas," said Daisy.

Mum sighed one of her usual sighs. "If you eat your peas, you can have some pudding," said Mum.

"I don't like peas," said Daisy.

"If you eat your peas, you can have some pudding and  you can stay up for an extra half hour."

"I don't like peas," said Daisy.

"If you eat your peas, you can have some pudding, stay up for an extra half hour and you can skip your bath."

"I don't like peas," said Daisy.

"If you eat your peas, you can have ten puddings,

stay up really late, you don't have to wash for

two whole months and I'll buy

you a new bike."

"I don't like peas," said Daisy.

"If you eat your peas, you can have 48 puddings,

stay up past midnight, you never have to wash again, I'll buy you two new bikes and a baby elephant."

"I don't like peas," said Daisy.

"If you eat your peas, you can have 100 puddings,

you can go to bed when you want, wash when you want,

do what you want when you want,

I'll buy you ten new bikes,

two pet elephants,   three zebras,   a penguin

and a chocolate factory."

"I don't like peas," said Daisy.

 "If you eat your peas, I'll buy you a supermarket stacked full of puddings,

you never have to go to bed again ever, or school

 again, you never have to wash,

or brush your hair,

 or clean your shoes,

or tidy your bedroom,

I'll buy you a bike shop, a zoo, ten chocolate factories,

I'll take you to Superland

for a week and you can have your very

own space rocket with

double retro laser

blammers."

"If you eat your peas, I'll buy you every supermarket, sweet shop, toy shop and bike shop in the world,

seventeen swimming pools,

you never have to go to bed again,

or go to school, or wash,

or brush your hair or clean your shoes,

or clean your teeth,

or clean your hamster out,

or tidy your bedroom,

or put the videos in yourself,

or get dressed,

I'll buy you Africa and ninety two chocolate factories, we'll move to Superland, you can have all the space rockets you want, I'll buy you the earth, the moon, the stars, the sun and... and... and...

...and a new fluffy pencil case!"

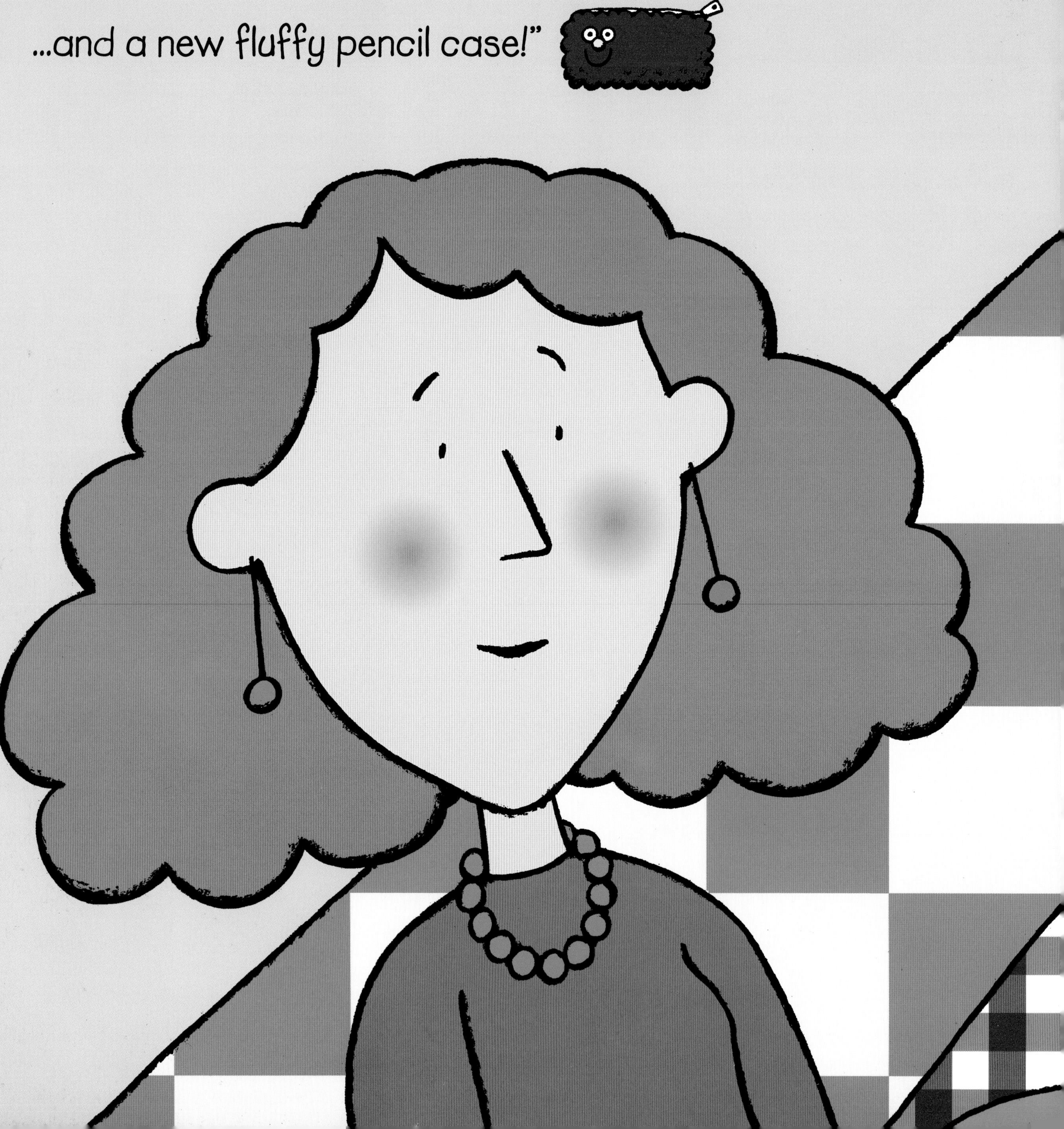

"You really want me to eat my peas, don't you?" said Daisy.
"Yes," said Mum.

"I'll eat my peas if you eat your Brussels," said Daisy.

Mum looked down at her own plate
and her bottom lip began to wobble.
"But I don't like Brussels," said Mum.

"But we both like pudding!"

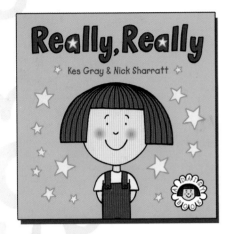

Really, Really
Kes Gray & Nick Sharratt

You Do!
Kes Gray & Nick Sharratt

Yuk!
Kes Gray & Nick Sharratt

006 and a Bit
Kes Gray & Nick Sharratt

With a free DAISY SPY KIT!

Come and play with Daisy at
Daisy Club
Kes Gray & Nick Sharratt
MEET DAISY
FUN STUFF
DAISY CLUB
GROWN-UPS
DAISY SHOP
www.daisyclub.co.uk

Kes Gray
Nick Sharratt
Double Trouble
Now with 8 pages of fun activities!

Tiger Ways
Kes Gray & Nick Sharratt

With free DAISY FINGER PUPPETS!

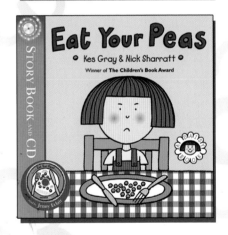

Eat Your Peas
Kes Gray & Nick Sharratt
WINNER of The Children's Book Award
STORY BOOK AND CD

A Bunch of Daisies
Kes Gray
Nick Sharratt

DAISY and the TROUBLE with **LIFE**
by Kes Gray
With a free DAISY BOOKMARK inside!

DAISY and the TROUBLE with **ZOOS**
by Kes Gray
Free Daisy BOOKMARK inside!

DAISY and the TROUBLE with **GIANTS**
by Kes Gray
Free Daisy BOOKMARK inside!

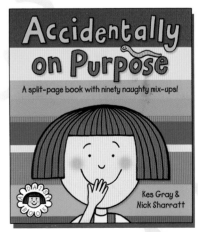

Accidentally on Purpose
A split-page book with ninety naughty mix-ups!
Kes Gray & Nick Sharratt

New longer Daisy story books!